W9-BKI-597

MONTIGUE
On the High Seas

Story and Pictures by
John Himmelman

Puffin Books

PUFFIN BOOKS
Published by the Penguin Group
Viking Penguin, a division of Penguin Books USA Inc.,
40 West 23rd Street, New York, New York 10010, U.S.A.
Penguin Books Ltd, 27 Wrights Lane, London W8 5TZ, England
Penguin Books Australia Ltd, Ringwood, Victoria, Australia
Penguin Books Canada Ltd, 2801 John Street, Markham, Ontario, Canada L3R 1B4
Penguin Books (N.Z.) Ltd, 182–190 Wairau Road, Auckland 10, New Zealand

Penguin Books Ltd, Registered Offices: Harmondsworth, Middlesex, England

First published in the United States of America by Viking Penguin,
a division of Penguin Books USA Inc., 1988
Published in Picture Puffins, 1990
1   3   5   7   9   10   8   6   4   2

Copyright © John Himmelman, 1988
All rights reserved

LIBRARY OF CONGRESS CATALOGING-IN-PUBLICATION DATA
Himmelman, John.   Montigue on the high seas / story and pictures by John Himmelman.   p.   cm.
Summary: After being flooded out of his home and swept out to sea,
Montigue the mole finds himself leading a crew of shipbound mice on a daring rescue.
ISBN 0-14-050789-2
[1. Moles (Animals)—Fiction.   2. Mice—Fiction.]   I. Title.
[PZ7.H5686Mo   1990]   [E]—dc20   89-36030

Printed in Hong Kong
Set in Baskerville

Except in the United States of America, this book is sold subject to the condition
that it shall not, by way of trade or otherwise, be lent, re-sold, hired out,
or otherwise circulated without the publisher's prior consent in any form of binding
or cover other than that in which it is published and without a similar condition
including this condition being imposed on the subsequent purchaser.

BOMC offers recordings and compact discs, cassettes
and records. For information and catalog write to
BOMR, Camp Hill, PA 17012.

This book is dedicated to my wife,
whose patience and creative advice has
helped me in every endeavor.
Thanks, Betz.

In a cozy hole by the sea, there lived a young mole. His name was Montigue.

Montigue loved his home. It was cool in the afternoons and warm in the evenings.

One day it began to rain. Soon the rain was coming down in buckets. By evening, Montigue's home was flooded. He had to find a safe place to spend the night.

Montigue swam and swam until at last he
noticed a funny-looking house propped on a
rock.

He was so tired that he fell into a deep sleep as soon as he crawled inside.

Montigue woke up rested and warm. It was a few moments before he realized that he had been . . .

. . . swept out to sea!

Poor Montigue drifted for days with nothing to drink except lime soda and nothing to eat but seaweed.

He grew lonely and bored as he stared at the horizon day after day. Then one morning, he noticed a dark shadow beneath him.

Suddenly, he was thrown into the air by a giant
humpback whale!

Montigue clung to the bottle as it slowly filled
with water and sank.

A passing fish, spotting an interesting meal,
swallowed the bottle, mole and all!

Before Montigue knew what was happening, the
fish was yanked up by a huge net. Montigue and
the bottle fell out of its mouth and onto the deck
of a ship.

Montigue looked up half-dazed and saw a giant
sailor looming over him. He was holding a giant
cat!

The cat leapt after him, but Montigue scuttled
into a hole. "Safe at last," he thought.
"What a funny-looking mouse," said a voice
beside him.

Montigue was surrounded by mice.
"What were you doing out there?" asked one,
nervously. "Don't you know that Barnacles the
Cat is trying to clear us all off this ship?"

Montigue began to tell them how he came to the
ship. He told of battling raging seas, riding giant
whales, fighting off mole-eating fish, and he told
them of the crash of his bottle ship.

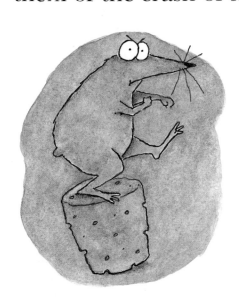

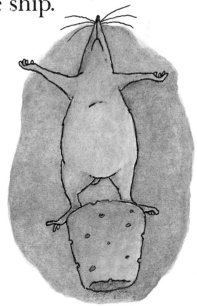

Just as he was coming to the end of his story, Montigue fell off his perch and knocked over a box of kitchen supplies.

When things settled down, thc mice cheered.
Montigue had given them an idea.

The mice scurried in every direction, collecting bits of cloth, rags, and other supplies.

Even Montigue got caught up in the fun.

They all worked together and soon their fleet
was launched.

The mice elected Montigue their captain. As
they glided over the sea, he began to enjoy the
thrill of guiding the ships through the waves.

In a few days, one of the mice shouted,
"LAND HO!"

When they were safely ashore, the mice carried
Montigue on their shoulders. They asked him to
live with them and he happily accepted. They
started building their homes right away.

Montigue loved his new home. It was cool in the afternoons and warm in the evenings. And now he had lots of friendly neighbors.

And if he ever felt the pull of the high seas, he still had his bottle and his sail.